Clean and Green Energy

Colleen Hord

ROURKE PUBLISHING

www.rourkepublishing.com

www.rourkepublishing.com

PHOTO CREDITS: Cover: © Mark Evans, © Lee Pettet, © elyrae; Title Page: © Murat Giray Kaya; Page 4: © Alexei Averianov; Page 5: © Catherine Yeulet; Page 7: © Cornelia Pietzsch, © anp © Christian Misje; Page 8: © acilo; Page 9: © Julia Nelson; Page 10: © newphotoservice; Page 11: © James Barber; Page 12: © pckane; Page 13: drobm; Page 14: © Steven Vona; Page 16: © maxfx; Page 17: © Bjorn Erlandsson; Page 18: © Goldmund; Page 19: © Wikipedia; Page 21: © Rhoberazzi; Page 22: © David Crockett

Edited by Kelli L. Hicks

Cover and Interior design by Tara Raymo

Library of Congress Cataloging-in-Publication Data

Hord, Colleen.
  Clean and green energy / Colleen Hord.
    p. cm. -- (Green earth science)
  Includes bibliographical references and index.
  ISBN 978-1-61590-300-9 (Hard Cover) (alk. paper)
  ISBN 978-1-61590-539-3 (Soft Cover)
  1. Renewable energy sources--Juvenile literature. I. Title.
  TJ808.2.H67 2011
  333.79'4--dc22
                              2010009640

Rourke Publishing
Printed in the United States of America, North Mankato, Minnesota
020111
01312011LP-A

www.rourkepublishing.com - rourke@rourkepublishing.com
Post Office Box 643328 Vero Beach, Florida 32964

Table of Contents

Energy

We use **energy** every day. Energy is the power that makes machines move or do work.

We use energy to heat our homes, dry our clothes, and to fuel the cars and buses that take us to school.

Clean and Green Energy

Clean and green energy is energy that is Earth friendly. Clean energy comes from the Sun, wind, and water.

Clean and green energy is **renewable**. Renewable energy is energy that won't run out.

Fossil Fuels

Some of the energy we use is not clean and green. Some energy pollutes the Earth's air and water.

Energy that pollutes the air and water comes from **fossil fuels**. Fossil fuels, like coal and oil, come from deep in the Earth.

Someday we will run out of fossil fuels. Scientists are working hard to find energy that is clean and green.

Solar Power

Solar power is one kind of clean and green energy. The Sun's heat is stored in solar panels. The solar panels use the Sun's heat to make **electricity**.

Think Green!
Another name for solar power plants is solar farms.

Some people have solar panels on their roofs. The solar energy heats up water for washing clothes and taking baths. The solar panels store up the Sun's heat so homes have electricity even on days when the Sun isn't shining.

Try This

Why Are Solar Panels Black?

To answer this question, let's try an experiment to see what color absorbs the most heat from the Sun.

Materials:
- 2 ice cubes
- 1 black piece of construction paper
- 1 white piece of construction paper
- A clock or timer
- A sunny day

Directions:
1. Find a sunny spot outside where you can set both pieces of paper side-by-side.
2. Place one ice cube on the black paper and one ice cube on the white paper.
3. Check the ice cubes every 5 minutes. Answer these questions:
   Which ice cube is melting fastest?
   Which color of paper is the ice cube on?

Results:
Now you know why solar panels are made from dark colored materials. Dark materials absorb the heat from the Sun better than light materials.

Wind Power

Have you ever seen what looks like giant pinwheels in a farmer's field? Some farmers are using their land for wind farms.

The wind spins the blades on the wind **turbine** around and around. A turbine is an engine that has blades that spin when water, gas, or steam passes through the blades. The spinning blades turn the wind into electricity.

Water Power

The movement of water also creates energy. Water that rushes over a dam into a large turbine makes electricity.

Capturing ocean waves is another way to make energy from water. The waves go through turbines in the ocean and electricity is made for homes and businesses.

Geothermal Energy

Geothermal energy is water energy that comes from deep inside the Earth.

The center of the Earth contains hot water and steam. Wells are dug deep into the Earth. The steam and water are pumped from the wells up to the Earth's surface to make energy.

Energy is all around us. We can use the Sun, wind, and water to make the clean and green energy we use in our homes and schools for many years to come.

Glossary

electricity (i-lek-TRISS-uh-tee): a form of energy caused by the motion of electrons and protons

energy (EN-ur-jee): power from coal, electricity, or other sources that make machines work

fossil fuels (FOSS-uhl FYOO-uhlz): coal, oil, or natural gas, formed from the remains of prehistoric plants and animals

geothermal energy (jee-oh-THUR-muhl EN-ur-jee): to do with the intense heat of the internal part of the Earth and its commercial use

renewable (ri-NOO-ay-buhl): power from sources that can never be used up, such as wind, waves, and the Sun

solar (SOH-lur): powered by energy from the Sun

turbine (TUR-bine): an engine driven by water, steam, or gas passing through the blades of a wheel and making it revolve

Index

Websites

www.eere.energy.gov./kids/

www.scholastic.com/actgreen

www.energystar.gov

About the Author

Colleen Hord lives on a small farm with her husband, llamas, chickens and cats. She enjoys kayaking, camping, walking on the beach, and reading to her grandchildren.